YOU CHOOSE...

BOOKS IN THE *YOU CHOOSE* SERIES

You Choose 1: The Treasure of Dead Man's Cove

You Choose 2: Mayhem at Magic School

You Choose 3: Maze of Doom

You Choose 4: The Haunting of Spook House

THE HAUNTING OF SPOOK HOUSE

GEORGE IVANOFF

RANDOM HOUSE AUSTRALIA

For my mum and dad. Thanks for everything. – G.I.

A Random House book
Published by Random House Australia Pty Ltd
Level 3, 100 Pacific Highway, North Sydney NSW 2060
www.randomhouse.com.au

First published by Random House Australia in 2014

Addresses for companies within the Random House Group can be found at www.randomhouse.com.au/offices.

National Library of Australia
Cataloguing-in-Publication Entry

Author: Ivanoff, George, 1968–
Title: The haunting of Spook House
ISBN: 978 0 85798 386 2 (pbk)
Series: You choose; 4
Target Audience: For primary school age
Subjects: Plot-your-own stories

Cover and internal illustrations by James Hart
Cover design by Christabella Designs
Internal design and typesetting by Midland Typesetters, Australia
Printed in Australia by Griffin Press, an accredited ISO AS/NZS 14001:2004 Environmental Management System printer

Random House Australia uses papers that are natural, renewable and recyclable products and made from wood grown in sustainable forests. The logging and manufacturing processes are expected to conform to the environmental regulations of the country of origin.

Ominous clouds loom above the creepy old two-storey house at the top of the hill. The boards are grey, the paint peeling and curling. Weeds grow in the gutters. The picket fence is falling apart. The gate leading to the overgrown garden has broken off its hinges.

You wonder if you should go in.

Your mind runs through what you know about this sad, ancient house . . .

No one has lived in it for years. Past residents have met with tragedy, misfortune – even death. You've done the research.

You know that in the 1800s, an archaeologist owned the house – until one day his wife came home to find him mummified.

You know that in the early 1900s, a

middle-aged man blew himself up in the backyard.

You know that in the 1960s, an eight-year-old boy was murdered by his insane nanny.

There was also something about a soldier mauled to death by dogs.

And your friends are pretty sure that the house is haunted – they even call it Spook House.

You, on the other hand, are not so sure it's haunted . . . and that's what has got you into this mess. You told your friends, Anna and Josh, that you didn't believe the ghost stories and so they dared you to go into the house.

So here you are, standing outside, wondering if you should go in. Anna and Josh haven't shown up to meet you like they said they would. Do you go in anyway?

If you decide to be bold and enter through the front door, go to page 8.

If you think it might be better to cautiously slip around the back, go to page 6.

Since your friends haven't bothered to show up, maybe you should just head home instead? Go to page 4.

You decide there's no point entering the house if Anna and Josh aren't here. After all, it was their idea.

You take a last look up at the house and begin to wander off.

As you glance about at the neighbouring houses, you see a man with binoculars. He's hiding in the frontyard of the house next door to Spook House, watching it from the shrubbery.

You wonder what he's up to.

Is your curiosity strong enough for you to stick around and investigate? If so, go to page 10.

If you'd rather go home and get an ice-cream, go to page 5.

You wander home and get yourself some ice-cream.

The next morning, there's a picture of Spook House on the front page of the newspaper. And there's also a photo of your friends, Anna and Josh. It appears that they alerted the police to a gang of criminals that was using the building as a hideout.

Police also arrested a man claiming to be a ghost hunter – but after jumping through a window, he disappeared into thin air.

It seems like you missed out on quite an adventure! If only you hadn't gone home for ice-cream, you too might have got your photo in the newspaper.

You decide to enter, to prove to yourself that there are no ghosts. But you don't like the idea of going through the front door. It seems too exposed.

So you walk around to the right side of the house. Cracked paving stones form a metre-wide path along the fence.

You take five paces down the path and stop at the first window. It's opened just a crack. You glance through the window to see some furniture covered in old sheets. It looks like the lounge room.

You think about going through the window.

But then a huge hairy spider scuttles across the wall and comes to rest on the sill, as if to guard it against entry.

If you'd like to avoid the spider and continue to the back of the house, go to page 14.

If you think climbing through the window might be more exciting, go to page 24.

You decide that the direct approach is the best, and march up to the entrance.

It's an oversized door, taller and wider than what you would find in an average house, and it looms in front of you. It has an odd, old-fashioned doorbell – the sort that you pull on rather than press. It's covered in spider webs.

You study it closely and wonder if there's a spider hiding in the dark crevice around the knob.

If you want to pull on the doorbell and risk a spider scuttling out over your hand,
go to page 18.

Otherwise you can just try opening the door – after all, the house is abandoned.
Go to page 16.

You casually pass by the shrubbery where the man with the binoculars is hidden. Then you lean up against a lamp post and spy on him.

He never once looks back in your direction. He is way too focused on watching Spook House.

You keep an eye on him for what seems like ages, but he does nothing other than stare through the binoculars. You start to get bored and are about to move off, when he rises up out of the bushes. Eyes still glued to the binoculars, he slowly walks sideways up to the front of his house and edges in through the door.

You observe the house for a little while longer. Just as you're about the leave, he emerges.

He's carrying some sort of electronic device – a bit like a cross between a mobile phone and sci-fi movie prop. And he's wearing high-tech goggles. Now you really are intrigued.

The man is no longer trying to conceal himself. He's standing out in the middle of his frontyard, staring at Spook House and occasionally looking down at the device in his hand.

Suddenly he ducks down. Anna and Josh come out of the house.

What were they doing in there?

Do you want to meet up with your friends and ask them what they've been up to?
Go to page 36.

If you'd rather stick around and find out what this weird guy's been doing,
go to page 20.

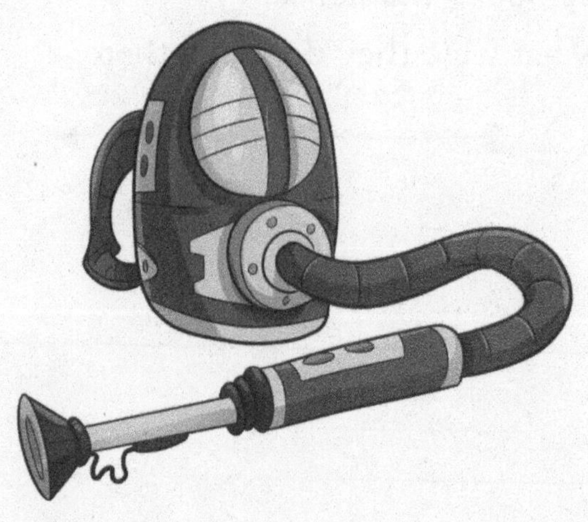

You throw yourself back out onto the paving stones. The window slams down with a loud bang. Another big hairy spider scuttles across the ground in front of your face.

You scramble to your feet and run down the passage, through the frontyard and out onto the street. You run all the way home and never go near that house again.

Your friends tease you about it for years to come, calling you . . .

The Chicken of Spook House!

You go along the path.

The backyard is large and overgrown with weeds. Ignoring it, you head straight for the door. It's unlocked. You open it and enter.

It's a kitchen – dusty and grimy. You walk through the inside door, into a hallway. There are closed doors on the left of the hall. You continue until you reach the front entranceway, where a large staircase leads up to the second storey. A little stone gargoyle sits on the end of the bannister.

The house is gloomy and spooky. Your footsteps echo around you as you walk.

Now that you're in here, you really should explore.

If you would like to go upstairs,
go to page 26.

If you'd like to try the nearest hallway door,
go to page 34.

You push the door open. It creaks loudly, the sound echoing through the house.

Your footsteps reverberate on the dusty floorboards as you step into the once grand entrance. A massive staircase dominates the area, spiralling up to the second floor. A little stone gargoyle sits on the end of the bannister. To the right is a hallway with closed doors, leading to a kitchen through which you glimpse the back door.

To the left, tucked away in the dark corner under the stairs, is a small doorway. You almost missed seeing it entirely. You wonder if it leads to the basement.

But which direction should you go?

If you'd like to explore upstairs, go to page 26.

If you'd like to check if the small door leads to the basement, go to page 32.

Or you can try one of the doors down the hallway – perhaps the second one. Go to page 34.

You pull on the doorbell . . . except that it's not a bell. It sounds like a foghorn. And it's LOUD!

No one answers. Not that you really expected anyone. After all, the house is abandoned.

So you push the door open. It creaks loudly, the sound echoing through the house.

Your footsteps reverberate on the dusty floorboards as you step into the once grand entrance. A massive staircase dominates the area, spiralling up to the second floor. A little stone gargoyle sits on the end of the bannister.

Tucked away in a dark corner under the stairs is a small doorway. The door swings open and a short stocky man marches out.

He wears overalls and heavy workboots, and is sporting a shaved head and a scraggly beard. He looks rather angry.

'You're trespassing on private property,' he barks.

You take a step backwards.

'Hold it right there,' he bellows, striding towards you.

Do you hold it right there? Go to page 29.

Or do you run? Go to page 47.

You want to keep watching this strange man with his goggles and device. But if your friends see you, they'll want your attention.

You dash into the man's frontyard and duck down behind a bush until your friends have walked off. Once they've gone, you decide to approach the man.

You come up behind him and say hello.

He jumps, drops his device, gives a squeaky scream and spins around. His eyes are magnified by the goggles, making him look a bit frog-like.

You ask him why he's watching the house.

'Ghosts!' he whispers, glancing from right to left, as if expecting someone to be listening in.

You stare at him.

'I am Josiah Samuel, ghost hunter,' he announces, puffing out his chest and standing taller – which isn't all that tall. 'I am renting this abode so I can be closer to that.' He points to Spook House.

You give him a sceptical look.

'You don't believe me.' He slumps sadly. 'That's fine. I realise that my appearance probably doesn't match most people's expectations of a ghost hunter.' He lifts up his goggles, straightens up again and stares at you with determination in his eyes. 'But let me assure you that I do hunt ghosts. And woe betide those that cross my path.'

Josiah crouches down to pick up his device. 'Now, I think it's time for me to start hunting. Excuse me while I prepare myself.'

He scurries away into his house. Moments later he reappears. Josiah has now got a box strapped to his back. It looks a bit

like a vacuum cleaner. It has a plastic hose attached to it, with the other end hanging from a hook on his belt.

'My containment unit,' says Josiah, patting the box. 'For trapping ghosts.' He lowers his goggles over his eyes. 'Once more, unto the breach!' Then he turns to you. 'Want to come?'

If you'd like to join this odd ghost hunter, go to page 37.

But maybe he's crazy? Perhaps it's safer to catch up with your friends instead? Go to page 36.

You slip off your shoe and slam the heel down on the spider.

Squish!

Spider guts splatter the front of your shirt.

You put your shoe back on and pull up on the window. It's old and stiff. You tug on it and, with a hair-raising screech of protest, the window finally opens.

You peer in. It seems as if no one's been inside the house for years. There's dust and cobwebs everywhere. Sheets are draped over all the furniture.

You hoist one leg up and over the sill. Then you hear a strange wheezing sound that makes you think of a gigantic monster's intake of breath.

The window slams right on top of you. Pain shoots through your skull and your vision blurs.

You push the window up with one hand, but it feels as if it's resisting, like it's trying to bite down on you. You can't hold it open much longer.

You only have a couple of sections to make your decision – in or out?

If all this is enough to scare you away, go to page 13.

But if your curiosity is stronger than your fear and you want to climb in, go to page 43.

Or perhaps you should climb out and try going through the back of the house? Go to page 14.

You approach the steps. Did that gargoyle just blink? You shake your head and slowly climb the staircase, the old wooden boards creaking beneath your feet.

You are halfway up when you hear movement from above. Footsteps?

You pause and listen. Everything is quiet again. You take a deep breath and continue.

You reach the second floor. There are three doors, all closed.

You move towards the first one. You reach out for the doorknob, but just before you touch it, a moaning sound comes from within.

You snatch your hand back and listen.

'Get out!' says the voice.

You take a sudden step backwards and trip over your own feet.

'Get out!' it repeats. 'Get out of the house. Run! Run away!' And then it laughs.

Your first impulse is to do as it says – to run away.

But what would your friends say if they found out that you had fled. After all, you don't really believe in ghosts – do you?

If you want to overcome your fear and open the door, go to page 71.

If you think it will be safer to leave, go to page 45.

Carefully, you prise out the brick and peer in.

To your surprise, you see a pair of glowing eyes gazing back at you.

Go to page 149.

You know you're in the wrong . . . entering a house that you have no permission to enter.

You try to explain that you thought the house was abandoned, but the guy cuts you off.

'Don't care,' he snarls. 'You shouldn't be here.' He balls his right hand into a fist and slams it into the palm of his left. 'If you know what's good for you, you'll turn around and walk out of here. You'll leave and never come back. You got that?'

'What's going on?' a voice calls from the staircase.

The man turns and shouts up the stairs. 'Oi! Get down here now.'

Your eyes widen as Anna and Josh emerge from the stairs.

'This is private property and you lot are trespassing.' He slams his fist into his palm again, wincing slightly but trying to hide it.

'We're sorry,' says Josh. 'We thought this place was empty.'

'Yes,' adds Anna. 'We just came in here to play a joke on our friend.' She points at you.

You ask them what they're talking about.

'You were so sure this place wasn't haunted,' says Anna. 'We were going to try to change your mind.'

'Yeah.' Josh grins. 'I was gonna jump out at you, wearing a sheet and mask.' He turns around. 'I left the costume upstairs. I'll go and get it.'

A heavy hand comes down on his shoulder and spins him around.

'The only place you're going is out,' says the angry man. 'Right now!'

'But . . .' begins Josh.

The man shoves him towards the door. 'No buts! OUT!'

The three of you stagger outside.

'Stay the hell away!' bellows the man, before slamming the door.

And so your Spook House adventure ends before it can truly begin.

You approach the door beneath the stairs and open it.

You see that it leads to a set of brick steps. Cautiously, you begin the descent.

There is a rectangle of light in front of you. And a sound – a soft, wheezing, snuffling sound. Some sort of animal, perhaps?

Slowly you go down, step by step, brick walls to either side of you.

You reach the bottom and peer through the doorway. The basement is stacked full of boxes. At the far end of the room is a trestle table covered in . . . dolls? Yes, that's what it looks like. Dolls!

In the centre of the space is a man in a chair, fast asleep. You realise that his snores are the source of the strange noise.

The man is wearing overalls and heavy

workboots. He is short and stocky, with a shaved head and a scraggly beard. He looks rather frightening. Who is he? What's he doing here?

You thought the house was empty. Now that you know it isn't, perhaps you should leave? *Go to page 5.*

But if your curiosity about the dolls and boxes gets the better of you, quietly sneak in for a closer look. *Go to page 51.*

You open the door down the hallway, and enter.

It's a small room – a cross between a library and a study. There's an old-fashioned writing desk up against one wall and a pair of antique swords hanging above it. Dusty, overflowing bookshelves line the walls. In the centre of the room is a tall glass display-cabinet.

You're about to take a closer look at the swords, when a movement at the corner of your eye catches your attention. The cabinet! Did something move inside it? Or was it just light reflected in the glass?

You go to look. There is a weird array of stuff on display – statues, carvings, framed pictures, dog tags and a wooden box. Your eyes are drawn to the box, which has intricate

patterns carved into the lid. You notice that the dust around it has been disturbed, as if it's been moved just a little.

You hear a noise above you and stop to listen. It's a creaking sound, like someone (or something?) walking around upstairs. But this house is abandoned, isn't it?

The sound stops. Was it your imagination? Or is there someone up there?

You glance at the swords on the wall.

If you want to take a sword and go upstairs to investigate, go to page 54.

If you'd rather stay where you are and check out the box, go to page 56.

You run over to your friends and ask them what they've been up to. It turns out they'd been waiting in Spook House so that they could play a joke on you. But you never went in. It seems they don't really believe the house is haunted either.

The three of you head home for ice-cream.

An hour later, your neighbourhood is rocked by a massive explosion. You switch on the TV to see the news. Spook House is a smouldering pile of rubble, and the strange man from the house next door is being arrested. As the police lead him away, he stares at the news camera from behind his goggles and mouths the word 'ghosts'.

Maybe the house really was haunted?

Josiah leads you to his backyard and indicates the fence.

'We shall scale the divide and enter via the back door.' He scurries halfway up, then turns to you, slightly out of breath. 'Stealth is of the utmost importance.'

He throws a leg up over the top and hauls himself to the other side, falling with a crash.

'I am unharmed,' you hear his voice call back.

You're beginning to wonder if this is such a good idea, after all. But you might as well go along.

You climb over the fence and follow Josiah to the back door.

You enter the kitchen. Long disused, the space is covered in dust and cobwebs. It leads out to a hall with three doors on the

left and an entrance way at the end, with a grand staircase.

Josiah consults his handheld device and walks into the hall.

'This machine measures paranormal activity,' he explains. 'And this house is off the scale.'

He's scuttling down the corridor now, pointing his device in all directions, getting more excited as he goes.

He stops in front of the staircase, a little out of breath, and examines the readings on his device.

'Let's see . . . where is the highest concentration?' He does a 360-degree turn, device held out in front of him. 'Three potentially high source locations. We have a concentration of evil upstairs. There is a time distortion in the lounge room. And a conglomeration of multiple sources in the study.'

He takes a long, deep breath and looks at you.

'Do you have a preference for which we investigate first?'

If you want to head upstairs,
go to page 60.

If you want to investigate the lounge room,
go to page 104.

If you want to check out the study,
go to page 125.

You reach for the door handle again. But your hand goes straight through it, chilling your fingers to the bone.

You're confused. You can't understand why you can't turn the handle. Is there something wrong with it?

You decide you'll have to break through the door – just like they do in the movies. You take a few steps back and then charge at it with your shoulder.

But there is no impact.

You shiver as you pass through to the backyard. It's like momentarily plunging into a pool of ice water.

You look around the overgrown yard. Without hesitating, you run along the side of the house and out onto the street . . .

But something isn't right. The street looks

similar to what you know, with some key differences. The newer houses aren't there. The older houses look newer. All the cars seem different. You have definitely stepped back in time!

You see two ladies with prams standing on the footpath, chatting. They're dressed strangely. And like the boy, they are almost see-through, as if they have faded in the sun. You run up to them and try to get their attention. But they appear not to see you. You shout at them, but to no avail.

Panic is now setting in. You see a girl riding a bicycle along the road. You jump out in front of her, waving and yelling. But she doesn't stop.

She rides straight into you . . . and then *through* you!

You double over. It's as if you've been pricked with a million ice splinters.

You get up and stagger off. Soon you're running. But no matter how far you go, you can't get warm.

You find yourself in a shopping centre. There are people everywhere.

A man bumps into you, his shoulder passing through yours. You feel a stab of cold pain.

Another person walks right through you. You fall over. People are everywhere . . . walking over you . . . through you.

You are overwhelmed by the cold. You can no longer move. Your mind fogs, your vision fades . . .

You enter an eternity of cold, dark nothingness!

You throw yourself into the room as you let the window go. It slams down with a loud bang that echoes through the house, and you fall flat on your face onto the polished floorboards.

You pick yourself up, rubbing at your sore head, and immediately try the window. It won't budge. It's as if the house has swallowed you up.

You study the room. Your eyes widen. The room is different – newer. No dust. No cobwebs. No sheets. Flames are crackling in the fireplace, giving the room a warm glow. But you feel cold! A shiver creeps up your spine.

Have you stepped back in time?

You hear the door creak and turn to look at it. It's standing open, but there's no one there.

You walk out into the entrance hall. A grand staircase arcs up to the second floor. A corridor to the right leads to an open doorway, through which you can see the kitchen and the back door. Perhaps you should leave?

You hear a door slam upstairs.

Do you want to go upstairs and investigate?
Go to page 69.

Or maybe it would be better to just get out of this creepy house before it's too late?
Go to page 58.

You dash down the stairs, out of the house and onto the street.

'Hey, wait!' calls a voice from behind.

You look over your shoulder to see your two friends, Anna and Josh, running from the house, front door wide open behind them. They are both laughing.

As they catch up to you, Josh starts moaning, 'Get out! Get out of the house. Run! Run away!'

You realise that they've set you up. That's why they weren't there to meet you when you arrived. Anna and Josh were already inside, waiting to play a joke on you.

You're a bit annoyed with them, but soon you can't help laughing as well.

As the three of you walk away, the front door to Spook House slams shut.

You spin around. Isn't the house meant to be empty?

From inside you hear an eerie moan. Or was that the wind?

You and your friends glance at each other and then bolt off down the street.

The sight of the angry man storming towards you is frightening.

You turn and run for the door. But in your hurry, you smash straight into it.

As your head hits the wood, everything goes black.

Go to page 48.

You hear voices in the darkness.

Your head hurts.

You can't move properly.

You open your eyes. You're lying on a cold concrete floor near some steps. Your hands and feet are tied up.

The bald guy is talking to a woman with blonde spiky hair wearing a red suit.

'We've got to get everything out of here,' says the woman. Her voice is frosty and businesslike. 'Someone might come looking for that kid. And the last thing we need is attention.'

'Sure thing, boss-lady,' the guy answers.

'Would you stop calling me that, Bruno,' demands the woman.

'Sure thing, boss-la– I mean, Ms Winters.'

'Now we must organise the removal of

the counterfeit boy-band merchandise. While we do that, I'll have a think about what we should do with our little intruder. We might have to . . . dispose of him.'

Bruno chuckles.

Dispose? Counterfeit boy-band merchandise?

You close your eyes, pretending you're still unconscious, as they turn towards you.

You hear Bruno and Ms Winters go up the stairs . . . and then the door slams.

Your eyes snap open. You struggle with your bonds, but your hands and feet are securely tied.

You manage to get into a sitting position and check out your surroundings. You're in a small brick-walled room – it must be the basement. There are boxes everywhere. At the far end is a table covered in dolls . . . boy-band dolls! There's a vent above it.

You push yourself up against the wall, bracing yourself so that you can stand up.

You look up at the stairs and wonder if you can make it all the way to the top with your hands and feet tied.

If you want to try climbing the stairs, go to page 74.

If you want to move over to the table with the vent, go to page 89.

You creep up to the first of the cardboard boxes and look in. Dolls!

You pull one from the box and examine it. It's a blond-haired boy in a t-shirt and dark suit.

You check the next box. More dolls. These are of a dark-haired boy in similar clothing, his hair long and floppy.

Recognition hits. One-Way Street! The hottest boy-band since No Direction.

But why is this basement full of One-Way Street dolls?

You look closer at the doll in your hand. It's not a very good likeness. And shouldn't he be wearing a white suit? Maybe it's a fake? And the man in the chair is a criminal?

At that moment you realise that the basement is silent. The snoring has stopped!

A heavy hand comes down on your shoulder, spinning you around.

'You shouldn't be here,' growls the man. 'You are in big trouble.' He pushes you towards the chair he's been sleeping in. 'Sit!'

You stumble into the seat, still clutching the boy-band doll.

The guy pulls out a mobile and lifts it to his ear.

'Yo, boss-lady,' he says. 'We got us a bit of a problem. Just found a kid poking around the basement.' He listens for a moment. 'Yep. So what do you want me to do?' He listens again. 'Search the house? Yep. I can do that. Yep. Never know . . . there might be others.'

He puts the phone away and looks down at you.

'Boss-lady is coming down to deal with you personally. So you stay put while I search the house. Got it?'

You nod.

He snatches the doll from your hands. 'And don't touch the merchandise.'

Doll in hand, he stomps up the stairs and slams the door shut. You race for the stairs but trip on a loose brick in the first step.

It looks like something might be concealed behind it.

If you want to inspect the loose brick, go to page 28.

If you'd rather go straight up to the door, go to page 75.

You grab one of the swords from the wall. Surprised by its weight, you accidentally drop it, but you pick it up again and head upstairs.

Did that stone gargoyle on the bannister just wink at you?

It's your imagination, you tell yourself as you slowly climb the staircase, the old wooden boards creaking beneath your feet.

There's another bannister gargoyle at the top. This one is grinning.

You take a deep breath and continue.

On the second floor are three doors, all closed. You approach the first one. You nervously reach out for the doorknob. Before you can touch it, a moaning sound comes from within.

You snatch your hand back and listen.

'Get out!' says the moaning voice.

You clutch the sword tighter.

'Get out!' repeats the voice. 'Get out of the house. Run! Run away!' And then it laughs.

Your first impulse is to do as it says – to run away.

But then you remember that you have a sword to protect yourself with.

Do you enter, sword in hand?
Go to page 78.

But if you think it might be better to drop the weapon and run away, go to page 45.

You open the cabinet door and take out the box.

The box is about the size of a bread loaf. You turn it around in your hands and notice that something's inside. You try to open it, but it's locked.

You glance into the cabinet. There is a key sitting in the dustless rectangle where the box had been sitting. You pick up the key and unlock the box.

You lift the lid, hoping for jewels or money. Instead you find ashes. Ashes! You wonder why anyone would keep this in a box. And then you realise – this is probably someone's cremated remains!

You're about to close the lid when you notice the ashes are glowing. Surely they can't still be hot?

As you stare at them, sparks begin to jump out at you. What's going on?

If your immediate reaction is to throw the box away from you, go to page 82.

If you're able to stay calm and gently place the box on the floor, go to page 80.

You head down the corridor towards the kitchen and the back door. You reach for the door handle. But your hand passes straight through it. You pull your hand back quickly. It's very cold, as if you've touched a block of ice.

You hear an eerie whisper from behind you.

You turn to see a young boy. He is transparent. A ghost! A real ghost! You swallow hard, trying to control your fear.

Dressed in shorts and a polo shirt, the boy is gesturing for you to follow him. He turns and runs back along the corridor and into the lounge room.

You rub your eyes and wonder if you imagined the ghost.

And then you remember your hand

passing through the door handle. Did you imagine that, too?

What is going on? What should you do?

If you want to follow the ghost boy back to the lounge room, go to page 86.

If you would rather try the back door again, go to page 40.

You point to the staircase. Josiah nods and leads the way up the steps to the second of three doors.

The two of you walk into a bedroom. It is sparse. There's a single bed, a wooden desk with a mirror, a stool and a cupboard.

Josiah sweeps the room with the device and checks the readings.

'The paranormal energy seems to be converging under the floor over there.' He points to the corner.

You crouch to examine the ground and discover a loose floorboard. You pull it up to reveal a moth-eaten teddy bear stuffed into a small hidey-hole.

'That's it!' cries Josiah. 'There's so much energy in that toy, it must have a ghost trapped inside it.' He lowers his voice.

'That happens sometimes . . . spirits get tied to physical objects that were important to them when they were alive.'

You examine the teddy bear. It is close to falling apart – the stitching is coming undone, one of its ears has fallen off, and bits of stuffing are poking out from a tear in its back.

'Place the toy on the floor and step back,' says Josiah, unhooking the plastic hose from his belt.

You notice a slight glow from the bear's stuffing. What could that be?

If you want to pull on the stuffing to check it out, go to page 83.

If you decide to follow Josiah's instruction and put the toy on the ground, go to page 62.

62

You drop the teddy bear on the floor and step back.

Josiah takes aim with the plastic hose and thumbs a switch on its side. It's like turning on a futuristic vacuum cleaner. There's a high-pitched humming sound and light spills from the end, engulfing the bear.

Through the toy's fabric a transparent shape emerges, which becomes distorted as it's drawn towards the hose. Even then, you can tell the form it takes is that of a woman.

She is dressed in a black skirt and jacket, with white shirt and gloves.

'Noooooo,' she screeches. 'What are you doing to meeeeeeeee?'

'Transferring you from your teddy bear to the containment unit on my back,' says

Josiah matter-of-factly. 'Thus ensuring that your evil spirit never has the chance to cause harm in this world.'

'But the children,' she screams. 'So many naughty children that need to be punished!' Her transparent form warps even further as she is sucked halfway down the tube. 'I must make them eat their brussels sprouts.' And then she's gone – trapped inside the containment unit.

'Oh, I think not,' says Josiah, flicking off the switch. The humming sound stops and the light fades. 'One down . . . lots more to go. Where to next?' He turns to face you. 'Time distortion in the lounge room, or the conglomeration of multiple sources in the study?'

If you want to investigate the lounge room,
go to page 104.

But if you prefer to check out the study,
go to page 125.

There's probably someone trapped in the room with the rattling door. You decide to go and open it, but then the rattling stops.

You hesitate a moment before trying again. Your hand seems to pass through the doorknob. You pull your hand back quickly. It's very cold, as if you've touched a block of ice.

You reach for the door once more . . . and it opens before you can grasp it.

Inside is a single bed. There's also a wooden desk with a mirror and a hairbrush, a stool and a cupboard. It's very sparse.

You walk in cautiously.

The door slams and you whirl around. There's a transparent woman standing by the door.

She is dressed in a black skirt and jacket, with white shirt and gloves. Her hair is in a

neat bun and she is clutching a teddy bear. She seems prim and proper, but there is a mad glint in her eyes. You think she looks like a demented Mary Poppins, and you suddenly remember the story about the nanny who murdered the boy.

'Oh, dearie me,' she says, her voice sounding distant. 'You should not be in here. This is 1962. And you're in my room.' She tuts. 'Very bad!'

You back away, mumbling that you've seen another ghost.

'I am no ghost,' she whispers. 'You're the ghost. A ghost from the future.'

You're about to protest, but she raises a finger to her lips and shakes her head.

'You've been naughty,' she hisses and takes a step forward. 'Naughty children need to be punished.' She inches closer.

The woman smiles, revealing crooked,

black teeth. 'I think I need to teach you some manners.'

She continues to advance, backing you into a corner. 'You probably don't eat your brussels sprouts either.' Her hand snakes out towards you. 'I'd make you eat them.' You gasp as her hand passes straight through you . . . into your chest. 'Brussels sprouts are good for you!'

You are racked by an icy chill, which spreads throughout the rest of your body. It's as if your blood is being frozen in your veins.

The nanny leans in close. 'Time to go nigh-nigh, you naughty, naughty child,' her harsh voice rasps in your ear.

Your eyes close and you fall into cold, dark nothingness.

You walk up the stairs to the second floor. There are three doors, all closed.

The handle on the middle door turns and the panel shudders. It's as if someone is trying to get out. You are about to investigate, when you hear an eerie whisper from downstairs.

You look down to see a young boy standing at the bottom of the steps. He is transparent. A ghost! A real ghost! You swallow hard, trying to control your fear.

Dressed in shorts and a polo shirt, the boy is shaking his head and gesturing for you to follow him. He turns and runs into the lounge room.

You rub your eyes and wonder if you imagined the ghost. Behind you, the door is still rattling.

If you want to check out the lounge room, to see where the boy has gone, go to page 86.

If you'd rather open the rattling door on the second floor, go to page 66.

You take a deep breath and open the door.

You peer into a dim and dusty bedroom. A child's bedroom. There is a single bed, a cupboard and a toy box.

You step inside, walking to the centre. The curtains are drawn, making the space shadowy and gloomy.

The door slams behind you. You whirl around and scream as you see a skeleton dangling from the door. You stumble backwards and fall to the floor. Your heart is pounding.

You hear a muffled giggle.

You get to your feet and wipe the dust from your hands. Something isn't right.

You take a closer look at the skeleton. It's made of plastic.

You look down at the ground and see scuff marks and footprints in the dust leading to the cupboard. Suddenly you know what's going on.

Carefully you unhook the skeleton from the door and tiptoe over to the cupboard.

As quickly as you can you yank open the door, throwing the skeleton inside and slamming it shut.

Someone in the cupboard starts shouting. You lean on the door to stop them from getting out. The screams become more frantic, and the banging from inside gets louder and louder.

The bedroom door opens and your friend Anna rushes in.

You step away from the cupboard, and your other friend, Josh, falls out. He's tangled up in a sheet.

You grin down at your friend.

Anna and Josh have been trying to scare you . . . but it's you who has scared them!

They are annoyed with you at first, but soon all three of you are laughing and joking around as you head down the stairs and out of Spook House.

More like Lame House!

You jump towards the stairs.

As you hop up onto the first step, you land on a wobbly brick. It shoots out from under your foot and you crash to the floor.

Every bone in your body feels like it's been jarred and you're certain that you've acquired a whole lot of bruises. But the fall has loosened the ropes that bind you and you manage to free yourself.

You're about to run up the stairs, when you realise you're being watched.

You blink and stare at the step with the missing brick. From within that dark space, a pair of glowing eyes gazes out at you.

Go to page 149.

You run up the stairs and try the door. It's locked!

You crouch down and look through the keyhole. He's left the key in it. You know exactly what to do – you've seen it before on TV. You rush back down and search for a pen and paper, which you find on the table.

You slip the paper under the door and use the pen to push the key out of the keyhole. It falls onto the paper, which you pull back underneath the door.

You're a bit surprised that it worked, but you unlock the door and head out.

'I thought I told you to stay put,' says the stocky guy, standing at the top of the main staircase. He's still holding the boy-band doll, which he's pointing at you.

You look to the front door.

'Don't bother,' he says. 'I locked it.'

He stalks down the stairs, whistling a One-Way Street song.

You dash for the hallway, hoping to escape through the back door, but he speeds up, taking two steps at a time.

You duck through the nearest door into a sort of study. There's a writing desk, lots of bookshelves, a glass cabinet and two swords on the wall.

You grab one of the swords and turn to defend yourself, just as the thug enters.

'You are becoming a bit of a problem,' he growls, throwing the boy-band doll at you.

At that moment, you swing the sword, decapitating the doll.

The thug looks sadly at the head as it rolls across the floor. 'Okay,' he says, sounding defeated. 'I guess I'll let you go.'

He steps backwards out of the room and

waves his arm for you to pass. But then he gasps and steps out of view. You hear a guttural scream.

Then all is silent.

If you want to use this chance to climb out of the window and out of Spook House, go to page 121.

But if you choose to find out what happened to the thug, go to page 119.

You fling open the door and race into the room, sword held out in front of you. The curtains are drawn, making the room shadowy and gloomy.

The door slams shut. Startled, you spin around to see a skeleton by the door. You charge at it with your sword, half closing your eyes as you do so.

The next thing you know, you're tangled up in the skeleton's bones, stumbling around the room, waving your weapon in all directions.

The cupboard door bursts open and a ghost emerges into the gloom. It's all billowing whiteness, with a grinning skeletal face.

You stumble forward into the creature, which screams and drops to the floor, the skeleton and sword falling on top of it.

You race out into the corridor, where you are surprised to see your friend Anna.

'What have you done to Josh?' she screams, pushing past you into the room.

Josh? What you saw wasn't a ghost?

Now you're scared that you might have hurt your friend. But you're also angry at being tricked.

If your ire is greater than your fear, leave your friends and go home. *Go to page 93.*

But if you're really worried about Josh, follow Anna into the room. *Go to page 91.*

You quickly place the box on the floor in front of you and stand back.

You are just in time, as a little shower of sparks erupts from the box. And in the dazzling blaze, a ghostly figure rises up – a tall man with an intense gaze, wearing a trench coat. As the sparks subside, he stretches and yawns.

'So good to be out of there. Oh, Mumsie, why did you have to put my ashes in a box?'

He stretches again and looks at you.

'My name is Gabriel Thurston von Chase the Third,' he announces, as if he very much likes the sound of his own name. 'Thank you for opening that box and giving me more room to move.' He bows low then straightens. 'Now, if I could beg a little assistance? As you may have guessed, I'm a ghost. So long as my ashes are in that box, I am tied to it. If you could perhaps tip them out, I'll be free to finish the task that was cut short by my untimely death.'

You look from von Chase to his box of ashes. Should you release him? Do you really want to set free a ghost into the world? He seems nice enough . . .

If you decide to do as the spirit asks and tip the ashes out, go to page 117.

If you think it might be safer to leave the ghost in the box for now, go to page 95.

With a yelp, you throw the box away from yourself.

As it hits the floor, it explodes in a shower of sparks.

When the smoke clears, you see that there is someone standing right where the box has landed – a tall man with an intense gaze, wearing a trench coat. But something's not right. You can see through him.

'Free!' shouts the man. Then he fixes you with his manic stare. 'And it's all thanks to you.'

The man starts striding about the room. 'So good to be out of that box. Oh, Mumsie, why did you have to put my ashes in there?'

He stretches and looks at you.

'Let me tell you about my KABOOM!'

Go to page 141.

Your curiosity gets the better of you and you pull the stuffing that's poking out of the old teddy bear.

The bear bursts apart and you jump back.

Amidst the cloud of stuffing and torn fabric stands the ghost of a woman.

She is dressed in a black skirt and jacket, and a white shirt with gloves. Her hair is in a neat bun. She seems prim and proper, but there is a mad glint in her eyes. You think she looks like a demented Mary Poppins.

'Oh, dearie me,' she says, stretching out her arms. 'So nice to be out of that mouldy old bear. It's been too long . . . much too long. There are so many naughty children in this world and now I'm back to dole out the punishment. And to make them eat their brussels sprouts!' She fixes you with

an intense gaze. 'I think I'll start with you. You've been naughty, haven't you, pulling the stuffing out of that toy. I'll have to punish you!'

She waves her arms, and the torn teddy-bear pieces rise into the air and reassemble themselves.

'Get out of the way,' orders Josiah. 'You're blocking me.'

You step back and look around. Josiah aims the plastic hose at the ghost nanny, and thumbs a switch on its side. It's as if he's turning on a futuristic vacuum cleaner. Light spills from the end and there is a high-pitched humming.

The nanny screeches and flies out of the way. She zooms across the room, Josiah trying desperately to train his ghost vacuum on her. She swoops under his feet and trips him over. But the heavy pack on Josiah's

back weighs him down and he's struggling to get up.

The nanny pounces on you, shoving the teddy bear into your face. Fur and stuffing are pushed into your mouth. You can't breathe! You try to fight her, but you can't seem to touch her ghostly form.

'I bet you never eat your brussels sprouts!' she hisses.

You fall to the floor. And still, she keeps smothering your face with the old teddy bear.

'Naughty children must be punished,' her harsh voice rasps in your ear. 'Time to go nigh-nigh!'

You gasp for breath . . . until consciousness slips away.

You follow the ghost boy into the lounge room.

'Help me!' His voice is an ethereal whisper. You can hear it, but it seems distant.

The boy looks about eight years old. He's standing in the middle of the room. He appears frightened.

'The nanny,' he says, his voice shaking. 'She's coming to get me.'

You remember reading about the boy who was murdered here in the 1960s. Could this be his ghost? You look around the room – still no dusts or cobwebs or sheets. Perhaps the boy isn't a ghost. Maybe you've gone back in time?

You ask the boy what year it is. He looks at you strangely before answering.

'1962.'

You hear banging sounds from upstairs. The boy looks even more frightened.

'She's going to punish me,' he says. 'And she's locked all the doors and windows so I can't get out!'

You run from the lounge room to the front door. You reach out to see if it's locked, but your fingers pass straight through it. You pull your hand back quickly. It's very cold, as if you've touched a block of ice.

You stare at your hand and try to think things through. And then it dawns on you. You realise that you must be a ghost in 1962 – a ghost of the future! Somehow, climbing through that window has sent you back into the past.

The banging continues upstairs.

Should you go through the front door and try to get help for the boy? Go to page 106.

But what can you do? You're just an apparition. Maybe you should climb back out the window and return to your own time? Go to page 147.

You jump across the room to the table with the vent above it.

You hop up so that you are sitting on the table, swing your feet up onto it and then use the wall to brace yourself so you can stand. Standing on the table, you can reach the vent.

You start yelling for help.

It's not long before your friends Anna and Josh arrive. They tell you that they've been hiding on the second floor of the house, waiting for you to come so that they can play a trick on you. When you didn't show, they started searching for you around the house. They saw a man and woman drive off in a car and then they heard you yelling.

Anna has a mobile phone with her, so she rings the police.

Go to page 144.

You run back into the room.

Anna is kneeling on the floor beside Josh. There is a sheet and a plastic skeleton mask next to him.

Josh is lying very still.

'I think he's dead!' sobs Anna. 'What are we going to do?'

You look at Josh. He's not moving. Could he really be dead? Maybe there's still a chance?

Anna has a mobile phone, so you decide to call for emergency.

It's not long before an ambulance arrives.

Josh is not dead – but he is badly hurt. The paramedics quickly get him onto a stretcher and rush him to hospital.

If you hadn't called the ambulance straight away, it might've been worse!

A week later, Josh is still recovering in hospital. You and Anna go to visit him. He apologises for setting you up and trying to play a trick on you. And you say sorry for hurting him.

Now that it's all over, the three of you can sit around and laugh about it. But you realise just how lucky you were. Josh could have been killed. It seems that you did make at least one good decision!

You rush down the stairs, out of the house and straight home.

That night you have strange dreams. Josh is chasing you with a sword. He is wrapped in a sheet and wearing the plastic skeleton mask. But as he runs after you, he changes. The sheet and the mask melt into a transparent, wispy nothingness.

Josh morphs into a real ghost.

You wake up in a cold sweat, heart thumping.

In the darkness you see a glowing shape by your bedroom door. It's an ethereal outline of Josh.

'You killed me,' he moans.

You killed him? But you didn't mean to!

Josh rises up into the air and floats towards you.

'So now I'm going to haunt you . . . for the rest of your life!'

He swoops down towards you. You close your eyes and your ears are filled with Josh's manic laughter and the sound of your own screams!

You agree to tip the ashes out, but as you reach for the box, you snap the lid closed. The ghost of von Chase disappears.

You pick up the container and it rattles in your hand.

'Traitor!' comes a muffled voice from inside. 'You're as bad as Mumsie! I'll get you for this. I'll make you go KABOOM!'

You quickly use the key to lock the box. It stops shaking.

Now, what are you going to do with the box? If you leave it here, someone else might find it and open it.

Then, you get an idea.

You race out of the house and all the way to the local shopping street. At the end of the street is a dingy little alley. And concealed at the end of this alley is a shabby little shop.

You came across this store a few weeks ago, by accident. There's no sign, but there's an assortment of weird things in the window – tarot cards, pentagrams, grotesque statues and all manner of occult objects.

This seems like a good place to get rid of the box.

You push the door open and enter. It's dark and gloomy inside. Tables and shelves overflow with dusty curiosities and books.

'Vhat do you vant, young person?' asks a woman with an odd accent, appearing behind the counter. She looks old – ancient, in fact. She is covered in beaded shawls and scarves, bangles and bracelets, rings and brooches, looking just like you would expect a mad gypsy fortune-teller to look like.

You step forward slowly and place the box and its key on the counter, quickly

retreating. Her eyes widen as she runs her hands along the lid.

You are about to launch into the story of the ghost in the box, when she fixes you with a determined stare.

'You vill listen to me, young person,' she says. 'I vill give you vone hundred dollars for this box.' She reaches into her pocket and pulls out two fifty-dollar notes, waving them in front of you. 'Take it or leave it!'

One hundred dollars! You didn't expect to get money for the box. You wonder if she'd still give you the cash if she knew about the ghost. Would she want a haunted box? Either way, you really should tell her . . . right?

⋙————————➤

If you think you should let her know about the ghost – and risk losing a hundred dollars – go to page 114.

But if you just want to take the money and run, go to page 112.

You run down the hallway, through the kitchen and out the back door.

You sprint the length of the backyard and clamber over the fence. You are halfway down the next yard when you hear an explosion behind you. You turn to look.

Flames erupt from the back door. But there's also movement at the top floor window.

The window is flung open and a face appears.

'HELP!'

You recognise the voice. It's your friend Anna. What's she doing up there?

A second figure appears next to her. It's your other friend, Josh. Why are they up there? They were supposed to have met you outside the house. Maybe they came in looking for you.

You head back towards the house to try

to rescue them. But before you can reach the fence, the entire house is consumed in an enormous explosion.

You are knocked off your feet.

Your ears are ringing and you are momentarily dazed as debris rains down around you. You groggily lift your head to see the ghostly form of von Chase float out of the smouldering rubble. His voice echoes through your head.

'How was that for a KABOOM?'

Above the ruined house, von Chase ignites into a ball of flame and disappears.

But he's not the only one who's gone. So are Anna and Josh.

You could have saved them . . . but, instead, you selfishly chose to save yourself – a burden you'll have to live with for the rest of your life!

You dash up the staircase yelling that the house is about to blow up.

As you reach the top of the stairs, two people run towards you. You are surprised to see that it's your friends, Anna and Josh. It turns out that they'd arrived at the house earlier, planning to play a trick on you.

All three of you head down the stairs. The door to the study explodes, spewing flames into the hallway and blocking access to the kitchen and back door. So you head for the front door instead. You hear more blasts behind you as you go.

You make it out into the yard as the entire house erupts. The force of the fire knocks you and your friends off your feet and onto the street.

Your ears are ringing and you are

momentarily dazed as debris rains down around you. You groggily lift your head to you see the ghostly form of von Chase float out of the smouldering rubble. His voice echoes through your head.

'How was that for a KABOOM?'

Above the ruined house, von Chase ignites into a ball of flames and disappears.

The ghost is gone and the house is destroyed . . . but at least you and your friends are okay!

You follow Josiah into the lounge room. In addition to the dust and the cobwebs, there are old sheets draped over all the furniture.

Josiah walks around the room, sweeping his handheld device back and forth, until he finally comes to a stop by the window.

'The time distortion centres around here,' he says. 'It might be a portal into another period in time.'

He opens the window and sticks the device through it. Then he pulls it back and studies the readings.

'Hmm. Nothing happened.' He scratches his chin. 'Maybe it's one-way.' He looks up at you, a twinkle in his eye. 'Don't suppose you'd mind heading back outside via the kitchen and then climbing in through this window while I monitor you?'

But what happens if the window *is* a portal to another time? Will you travel into the past or the future? Will you be able to return here?

If you're willing to do as Josiah requests, go to page 130.

But if you think it's too dangerous, go to page 127.

You take a deep breath and a step back . . . then run at the door.

You shiver as you pass through it. It's like plunging into a pool of icy water.

You look around. The street seems similar to what you know, with some key differences. The newer houses aren't there. The older houses look newer. The cars look different. You definitely have stepped back in time!

You see two ladies with prams standing on the footpath, chatting. Like the boy, they are insubstantial, as if they have faded in the sun. You run up to them and try to get their attention. But they can't see you.

You try to tap one of the women on the shoulder, but your hand passes through her. You stagger back and clutch your hand. It's so cold it hurts!

Your heart pounds as you realise you could be trapped here.

You have a sudden desire to see your own house. It's an old building that was constructed in the 1920s, so it will exist in 1962. But what good would that do?

Maybe you should try to help the boy? There's a police station just a few blocks away. Perhaps you should go there?

If you want to head to the police station, go to page 110.

If you'd rather see your own home, go to page 108.

You run all the way to your house.

It hasn't changed much.

You walk up the drive and to the front door. There is rippled, stained glass to either side of the entrance instead of the clear panels you're used to, so you can't see in.

You can't help yourself – you feel the need to venture inside. You take a deep breath, close your eyes and step through the door.

Again, it's like plunging into ice water. Only this time, it's much worse. Your legs buckle, your head spins and you fall forwards.

You open your eyes to find yourself on the floor of your present-day house. The front door is open. There are clear glass panels to either side of it. Your cricket bat is leaning in the corner.

You've returned to your own time! Or maybe you never left? Perhaps you imagined it all?

But then, why do you feel so very cold?

Having made up your mind, you run all the way to where the police station should be.

And it is there! Although it's a different building, an older one.

The door opens and a man walks out. Quickly you slip through before it closes.

Inside, you try to catch the attention of the policeman behind the counter. You call out to him, you jump up and down, you wave your hands right in front of his eyes . . . but he continues reading his newspaper.

You shout in the policeman's ear out of sheer desperation. He looks up, thoughtful, then goes back to reading the newspaper.

You try again, getting as close to him as possible. As you shout, your lips pass through his ear. You fall backwards, your

lips blistering with the cold . . . but the policeman looks up, concerned.

'Who's there?' he calls out, standing up and walking around the counter. He opens the door and peers into the street before shaking his head and returning.

As you get to your feet an idea forms in your mind. Perhaps if you stepped into the policeman, occupied the same space as him, you might be able to get him to listen. But what would happen to you if you did? Would you freeze completely?

If you think that helping the boy is worth the risk, go to page 145.

If you're too scared of the consequences, maybe you should go back to your previous idea of seeking out your house? Go to page 108.

You snatch the money out of the woman's hand and bolt out of the shop.

You're halfway down the street when the shops are rocked by a massive explosion. You look back to see a burst of flame spew from the alley, followed closely by the apparition of von Chase.

You run!

'Traitor!' you hear von Chase screaming behind you. 'I'll make you pay. I'll make you go KABOOM!'

You put on a burst of speed as the pavement to the right of you explodes. Sparks rain down on you as you run, dodging from side to side.

You race back the way you came, passing Spook House. You notice that the fireworks have ceased. You look back over your

shoulder to see that von Chase is no longer pursuing you. He is circling above the house.

'KABOOM!' he screeches. 'I must complete my mission to be free.'

He swoops down to the house and disappears through the roof.

Seconds later, the entire house erupts. The force of the blast knocks you off your feet.

Your ears are ringing and you are momentarily dazed as debris rains down around you. You groggily lift your head to see von Chase float up from the smouldering rubble. His voice echoes through your head.

'How was that for a KABOOM?'

Above the ruined house, von Chase ignites into a ball of flame and vanishes.

The ghost is gone . . . and you are safe!

At least, you hope so . . .

Before the shop owner can give you the one hundred dollars, you tell her about the ghost of von Chase trapped with his ashes in the box.

The woman's eyes grow even wider as you recount the story. You're half expecting them to pop right out of their sockets. *That would be gross but interesting*, you think.

'Vell, vell, vell, young person,' says the woman, drumming her fingers on the counter. 'That changes everything.'

There goes the one hundred dollars, you think to yourself.

The woman reaches under the counter and brings up a wad of cash held tightly together with a grubby rubber band. She slaps it down on the counter.

'For a trapped ghost, I am villing to give you vone *thousand* dollars. Take it or leave it!'

You stare at the money for a moment, finding it hard to believe your luck. You reach for it and ask what she plans on doing with the ghost.

The woman slams her hand down on the cash and glares at you.

'There is no money for qvestions,' she hisses. 'You vant the money, you vill ask nothing. Yes?'

You nod.

'Good decision, young person,' she says, taking her hand off the bundle of notes. 'Take money and go. Yes?'

You grab the money and run.

By the end of the day you've got yourself a new bike, the latest computer game and a tub of quadruple-choc ice-cream. And

you've forgotten all about Gabriel Thurston von Chase III and Spook House.

You carefully pick up the box, the ghost of von Chase hovering above it, and tip the ashes out.

The ashes rise and swirl around the room as if blown about by wind.

'Free!' shouts von Chase as he flies about the room, swooping up and down until he comes to rest in front of you. He fixes you with his manic stare. 'And it's all thanks to you.'

He spreads out his arms and spins, his trench coat flapping around his legs.

Go to page 141.

Cautiously, you step through the door.

Something strikes out at you, knocking you to the floor. The sword slips from your fingers and skitters to the base of the stairs.

You look up to see the thug standing over you.

'I can't believe you fell for that,' he chuckles. 'Boss-lady ain't going to be happy with you.'

'And the police aren't going to be happy with you,' says Anna.

You and the thug look in surprise towards the stairs. Your friend Josh is holding the sword, while Anna is holding up her mobile phone.

Soon the police arrive.

It turns out Josh and Anna had come into the house earlier, intending to play a joke on you. Given that they've just come to your rescue, you think you might forgive them for that.

Go to page 144.

You dash to the window and yank it open.

The thug comes running back into the room.

'So much for my little trick,' he growls as he lunges for you. But he steps on the decapitated doll's head, pitches sideways and crashes to the floor.

You throw yourself through the window and run . . . straight to the police station.

Go to page 144.

You slip the key into the lock.

'No!' shouts Josiah.

Startled by his shouting, you drop the box. It springs open, strewing ashes all over the floorboards.

There is a blaze of sparks and a waft of smoke, which clears to reveal the ghost of a tall man with an intense gaze, wearing a trench coat.

'I'm free!' shouts the transparent man. 'Free to make a KABOOM!'

Josiah flicks the switch on the containment unit and aims the hose at the ghost. But the ghost zooms across the room.

'You can't catch me,' he shouts. 'Time for the fireworks.'

The ghost flings his arms out. Sparks explode from his fingertips, setting books

and shelves aflame. Josiah tries to trap the ghost, but he streaks out of the room and up the staircase, his voice echoing around the house: 'Time for a big KABOOM!'

'I'll get him,' calls Josiah, chasing after the ghost. 'You leave the house.'

You don't need to be told twice. You run down the hallway, through the kitchen and out the door.

You sprint the length of the backyard and clamber over the fence. You are halfway down the next yard when you hear an explosion behind you and feel a wave of heat. You turn to look.

Flames are erupting from the back door of Spook House. Windows are shattering. And then the entire house detonates. The force of the blast knocks you off your feet.

Your ears are ringing and you are momentarily dazed, as debris rains down

from above. Josiah's charred containment unit smashes to the ground beside you, missing your head by centimetres.

You look at the unit, then at the rubble of the house, then back at the unit. You wonder if Josiah managed to capture the ghost before he and the house went KABOOM. Just to be certain, you take the unit next door to Josiah's house . . . and bury it.

You follow Josiah into the study.

It's a small room. There's an old-fashioned writing desk up against one wall, a pair of antique swords hanging above it. Dusty, overflowing bookshelves line the walls. In the centre of the room is a tall glass cabinet.

With the device held out in front of him, Josiah heads straight for the cabinet. There is a weird array of stuff on display – statues, carvings, framed pictures, dog tags and a wooden box.

'All the paranormal traces are in this cabinet,' says Josiah, studying the readings. 'Let's see. The box. The Egyptian statue. The dog tags.'

Josiah steps back, unhooks the plastic tube from his belt and stands at the ready.

'Take them out, one by one. And be careful. Who knows what ghostly horrors lurk in each of these objects?'

You step up to the cabinet and peer in. Which shall it be?

If you pick the wooden box, go to page 133.

If you pick the Egyptian statue, go to page 138.

If you pick the dog tags, go to page 136.

You're not sure you want to go climbing through a potential time portal. So you suggest it might be better if Josiah does.

'Oh!' His eyes widen, magnified to even greater proportions by the goggles. 'Oh ... I don't think that would be wise ... because ... you see ...' He holds up his device. 'I need to monitor what happens. And record everything to study later.'

You point out that you could hold the machine for him while he climbs through the window from outside.

'Oh. Yes, I suppose you could.'

He tentatively hands you the device and slowly heads for the door.

A few minutes later Josiah is looking in through the window. He gives you a half-hearted wave and adjusts his goggles. He

places his hands on the windowsill and tries to climb through. The containment unit on his back knocks into the window frame and he falls backwards onto the ground outside.

'I am unharmed,' you hear him call out.

He pops back into view, now without the unit on his back. He again places his hands on the sill and throws a leg up and over. Losing his balance, he propels himself through the window . . .

And vanishes.

You wait for what seems like ages, but he doesn't reappear. So you head outside.

You discover that the window is shut and that, no matter how hard you try, you can't get it to budge. You run back to the lounge room. From inside, the window is still open.

You take a closer look at the window and

see something scratched into the paint on the frame. Words . . .

TRAPPED IN 1962!

You're rather excited about the possibility of going through a time portal. You race outside and look in through the window.

'Okay,' Josiah calls out to you. 'Climb through.'

You hoist one leg up and over the sill. You are halfway over when you hear a strange wheezing sound that makes you think of a gigantic monster's intake of breath.

Then the window slams down on you. Pain shoots through your skull. Your vision blurs.

You push the window up with one hand, but it feels like it's trying to close on you. You can't hold it open much longer.

'Stop!' You hear a distant voice calling. 'No.'

Is that Josiah? Should you climb back out?

The window suddenly feels heavier. It's bearing down on you, as if trying to bite you in half. You slip and start to fall into the lounge room.

But at the last second, a hand grabs you and pulls you outside.

The window slams shut!

You fall onto the paving stones and look up at Josiah. He is out of breath.

'The readings . . . as you were climbing over . . .' he pants. 'The portal was too weak. If you were to go through, only a shadow of yourself would have made it. You would have been a ghost in another time.'

Josiah unhooks the plastic hose from his belt and points it at the window. He thumbs a switch on its side, and the ghost vacuum cleaner springs into life. Light spills out over the window, and there is a high-pitched humming.

A ghostly image of the window is sucked through the tube.

'Now,' says Josiah, 'onto the next paranormal hotspot.'

But you shake your head. You've had enough ghostly activity for one day. You say goodbye to Josiah and head off.

As you're walking home, the right side of your body begins to tingle. Your right side? Wasn't that the side that went through the portal before Josiah rescued you?

You hold up your hand and look at it. Is it just a little less substantial? Could it be fading away into the past? Or is it just your imagination?

You lift the wooden box out of the cabinet.

There is a key underneath it. So you pick that up as well.

The box is about the size of a bread loaf, with intricate carvings across the lid. You turn it around in your hands and realise there's something inside.

'Place the box on the floor and step back,' instructs Josiah.

You know you should do what Josiah asks, but you're also curious about what's inside.

If you want to put the box down, go to page 134.

But if you want to use the key to open the box, go to page 122.

You place the box on the floor, with the key on top of it, and step back.

Josiah flicks the switch on the side of the hose and the containment unit hums into life. Light streams from the hose to the box, and a ghostly figure is slowly drawn out of it. It is an elongated and distorted image of a man in a trench coat.

'KABOOM!' shouts the ghost. 'I must have my KABOOM!'

Quickly, it is sucked up and you wonder what the ghost was shouting about.

'Well, that was easy,' says Josiah, turning off the unit. 'Next!'

You're feeling confident now. You saunter over to the cabinet to select the next object.

If you want to pick up the Egyptian statue, go to page 138.

If you want to go for the dog tags, go to page 136.

You grab the dog tags from the cabinet. They're hot!

You drop them to the floor, where they sizzle and smoulder, burning a hole.

As the dog tags fall through the scorched floorboards, Josiah aims his containment unit. But he's not fast enough.

Ghostly dogs leap from the hole, flames licking their heels. They have blazing eyes, smoking nostrils and rancid breath. Are they the hounds of hell?

You back up against the desk and remember the swords hanging on the wall. You quickly snatch one off the wall and hold it up defensively.

One of the hounds stops before you, glaring at you with its fiery eyes. The others set upon poor Josiah, jaws closing upon his

arms and legs, and drag him screaming into the flaming hole.

The remaining dog snarls at you, baring its teeth, then it too disappears into the hole.

You drop the sword and run – out of the house and back home.

You never speak of your experience with anyone. And from that day on . . .

You will always be scared of dogs!

You grab the statue from the cabinet. But it's made of stone and heavier than you expect. It slips out of your hands and cracks in half as it hits the floor.

The entire room shimmers.

Two ghostly figures appear – tall and burly, with dark skin and bulging muscles. They wear golden loincloths and headdresses. One of them grabs you, pinning an arm behind your back. The other restrains Josiah before he can activate his containment unit.

The room continues to shimmer.

Two stone altars appear. Between them is another ghostly figure. Although shorter than the other two, he wears a jackal headpiece that makes him appear taller.

He has a bowl of smouldering incense in one hand and a hook in the other.

You think back to what you've read about ancient Egypt. Didn't they pull people's brains out through their noses prior to mummification? Is that what they're going to do to you?

You struggle . . . but it's no use. Your ghost-guard is too strong. You watch as the jackal-headed man waves the bowl of incense under Josiah's nose. His eyes roll up and he collapses into the arms of his guard, who places him onto one of the altars.

You're next.

You can smell the sickly sweet odour as the jackal-man approaches. He moves the incense bowl in front of you and your mind fogs over, filling with indistinct images of mummies and brains in jars.

You try to fight the fog. But it's no use.

Consciousness slips away and you close your eyes . . . in preparation for mummification.

'I died whilst preparing my greatest endeavour . . . my biggest KABOOM.' The ghost leans towards you in a conspiratorial way. 'Slight miscalculation with the gunpowder ratios,' he adds with a lowered voice before returning to normal volume. 'I was intending to blow up my dear old Mumsie and her house. And now I'm out of that box, I can complete my mission. I'll finally get my KABOOM! You see, I'm stuck here as a ghost unless I can finish off what I was trying to do when I died. Once I've done that, and my soul is at peace, I can cross over to the other side.'

He thrusts out his hand towards the glass cabinet. Sparks shoot from his fingertips and the cabinet shatters.

'And my ghostly powers will make things so much easier.'

He sweeps his hand in an arc and books erupt from the shelves, bursting into flame as they hit the floor. 'What do you think of that, Mumsie?' he shouts at the ceiling. Then he grins your way.

'Now then, my friend. Since you were kind enough to free me, I'll grant you a few minutes to vacate the premises before I begin.'

You stare at him.

'Well, go!' he shouts at you. 'Shoo! Skedaddle! Or you'll end up going KABOOM along with this house.'

You don't need further encouragement. You bolt from the room.

In the entrance hall you hear a sound from above and glance up the stairs. You see

a figure run across the landing. Someone's up there!

If you decide to go upstairs to warn whoever it is that the house is about to explode, go to page 102.

But if you're more interested in saving yourself, go to page 99.

The police catch the criminals and confiscate the counterfeit products. The dolls were fake merchandise for the hottest boy-band on the planet – One-Way Street.

The band is so grateful for your help that you get given all their albums, as well as tickets to their next concert. There's even talk about you being in their next music video.

How cool is that?

Before you have time to change your mind, you step into the spot where the policeman is standing.

You gasp! You are so cold that you are unable to breathe. Your blood feels like it has frozen in your veins.

In your mind you picture the young boy calling for help. You picture the house and how to get to it.

The policeman steps away, leaving you shivering and unable to move. With a determined expression, he marches out of the station.

You still haven't taken a breath. You're still freezing. You're still shivering.

You close your eyes. Your legs collapse beneath you and you hit the ground.

When you open your eyes, you see two policewomen staring down at you.

You sit up to find yourself in the present-day police station.

Moments later an ambulance arrives and you are taken to hospital. The doctors check you out and say that everything is fine.

After your parents have brought you home, you go online and do a search for the 'Nanny Murder' of 1962. Nothing. It seems as if it never happened. So you do a search on the address of Spook House and finally find a newspaper article. The nanny did try to murder the boy. But a passing policeman had heard him screaming and burst into the house just in time to save him.

So you really did go back in time!

And you saved that boy's life!

You race to the lounge room, past the ghostly boy and to the window. You try to yank it open but it won't budge.

You suddenly realise that, unlike the front door, you're able to touch the window. More than ever, you're convinced that this is your way back to the present day.

Despite your efforts, the window will not give.

You look around the room for something with which to smash the glass. You pick up a little footstool and lift it up over your head.

'Nooooooo!' pleads the ghost boy.

You throw the stool with all your might.

It smashes through the glass.

The boy screams and disappears. Everything around shifts and blurs.

The room is old again – covered in dust

and cobwebs; the furniture draped in old sheets.

You approach the broken window and try it. It opens easily.

You climb out of the window and head straight home. You never go near Spook House again.

You scream and back away.

You watch in disbelief as a transparent woman squeezes out through the hole. It's a ghost! A real live ghost! Well, a real dead ghost!

The woman is short, with cascades of frizzy sandy-coloured hair. She's wearing blue jeans, a red cowboy shirt with gold tassels, and boots – bright red leather cowboy boots with gold and silver stars down the sides.

Amazingly, this ghost woman has a ghost guitar slung on her back.

'Well, hello there, ya'll,' she drawls in what sounds like a fake American accent. 'My name's Betsy-Lee Amber Howling.'

You stare at her.

'Ya'll okay there?' She looks at you. 'Kitty-cat got your tongue? Well now, I know just

how to cheer ya'll up and bring a smile to that sad-sack face.'

With a shake of her shoulders, she swings her guitar round to her front and starts strumming. It's a sad, mournful tune. And then she starts singing . . .

'Oh, I had a hard life, yes I did.

My boyfriend dumped me and my doggy hid.

My mommy died and my daddy ran,

Then there came a flood that burst the dam.

Oh-oh-oh,

Woe is me!'

Your eyes are wide with horror. Betsy-Lee Amber Howling is the ghost of a country-and-western singer. And not a very good one.

You interrupt her singing to ask for help. You tell her about the criminals and their counterfeit boy-band merchandise.

The mention of a boy-band sends Betsy-Lee into a frenzy. She streaks about the room, overturning boxes and smashing dolls as she screeches.

'Don't ya'll talk to me about boy-bands. I hate boy-bands! I was number-one on the charts until that No Direction boy-band came along and stole my rightful place. And that's when all my misfortunes began.'

With a strum of her guitar, the boy-band dolls on the table begin to shake. With another strum, their heads explode.

Betsy-Lee laughs like an insane banshee and continues strumming on her guitar. Box after box of merchandise explodes in an eruption of plastic and fake smiles. As country-and-western music fills the air, bricks shake loose from the walls and stairs. The door rattles and bursts off its hinges.

You realise there's no reasoning with the furious ghost of a hard-done-by country-and-western singer, so you race up the stairs and out of the house.

On the street you spot your friends, Anna and Josh. You join them and watch as the house collapses in on itself amidst a crescendo of wailing guitar music.

'What happened?' asks Anna.

You look from the rubble of the house to your friends and back to the rubble. You realise that they'll never believe you.

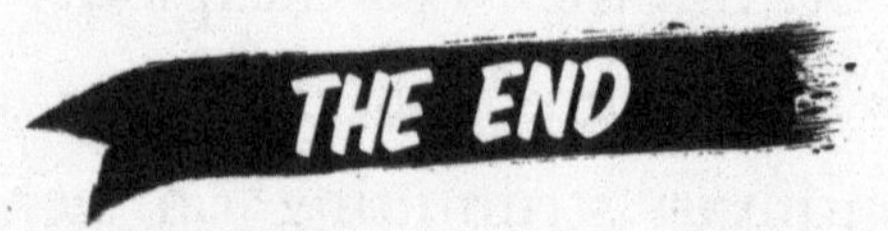

ABOUT THE AUTHOR

George Ivanoff is an author and stay-at-home dad residing in Melbourne. He has written over 70 books for kids and teens, including the Gamers trilogy. He has books on both the Victorian and NSW Premier's Reading Challenge lists, and he has won a couple of awards that no one has heard of. As a kid he loved reading interactive books, where he got to make decisions about the direction of the story. Now he is ridiculously happy, having the opportunity to write that type of book. He has had more fun plotting and writing the *You Choose* books than pretty much anything else . . . and he hopes you have just as much fun reading them. George drinks too much coffee, eats too much chocolate and watches too much *Doctor Who*. If you'd like to find out more about George and his writing, check out his website: georgeivanoff.com.au

YOU CHOOSE...

AN EXCITING SERIES OF INTERACTIVE NOVELS FOR THE HIGHLY ADVENTUROUS. READ IF YOU DARE! MISTAKES WILL COST YOU DEARLY!

COLLECT THEM ALL!

Loved the book?

There's so much more stuff to check out online

AUSTRALIAN READERS:

randomhouse.com.au/kids

NEW ZEALAND READERS:

randomhouse.co.nz/kids